YESTERDAY
WILL
BREAK
YOUR
HEART (1)

ALCALY
LO

To be around you
Is so-oh right
You're sheer perfection

Here is Juliet at the end of your shift and a little before hers. A Groundhog Day kind of night: solo northbound Georgia Avenue bus ride, Kantouri Fried Chicken to go, a little writing before bed if the spirit so moves you. "Give in, baby." Her hunger alone is more than you've gotten over many years from E.

"To what?" you ask, as if you don't already know, as if your hunger doesn't dovetail with her own.

She leans in, says it with a kiss: "To me, dummy. Us."

You have just received word that Anaëlle, warm and tender Anaëlle, is getting married. Is she your

1

"one that got away?" Too soon to say. It doesn't hurt, though. It doesn't hurt at all. But you know the drill: Pain and sadness and regrets take their sweet time but kick in with both feet and a vengeance they will, kick in they always do. Soon enough you'll be a mess. Inconsolable, forlorn, broken down. Sidelined, days bleak, white nights. Scrambled heart, stomach in eights, mind gone. On Lonesome Row, permanent frown, permafrost you. Swearing innocence just like the rest of them fools. Pining for the sweet yesterdays you all but threw away. What to do but keep your screwface on? *Pretender / Pretender / You better surrender*.

You wished Anaëlle well. "He meets my requirements" is how she described her reasons. Foundation enough to build upon? you pondered. Better than Cupid's arrow, Porgy and Bess, matching tattoos, fire and desire, a beach wedding, a Vegas honeymoon? Against bad odds, sandstorms, hurricanes, gale force winds, five-alarm blazes, twenty-foot waves, evil omens, locust swarms, climate change? Anyway, long story short, Anaëlle is out, out for good, good as gone. And it doesn't hurt. Not right now. Not at all. While you and she had feelings for each other, there was something lacking on your side from the get-go. You knew it. She knew it. Your whole world knew it. Like punching in, but barely. Like going through the motions with no predisposition for the game, killer instinct, trademark move, whiz-bang footwork, downfield vision, touchdown dance, sixth sense, gusto, intuition, jubilation. And it showed. *Look at us now / Will we always be together? / Who's to say?* You were both wounded early in life, but that's not what brought you and Anaëlle together, that wasn't enough to light the fire under your feet, make the crowd go wild, turn you into the best that ever did it, get you that ring, secure your Hall of Fame spot. No. That one is Sabine's whole entire story. That honor belongs to no one but Sabine.

Her names for you would change with the times, the moons, and her many many moods, but the first thing Sabine ever called you was Silver Surfer. It fired you up, lifted you, launched you straight into Orbit One. Before you knew it you were hurtling out of your comfort zone, deep into the uncharted, the unfamiliar, the unknown. "I get a good feeling," she said, "whenever I look at you."

What can you possibly know about entanglements at 15 (you) and 16 (she)? Long before it became a thing, you were misunderstood, a purported Rude Boy, a skater who stuck mostly to self. Sabine had everything going for her: hazel eyes, freckles, a Marylin mole that never stayed in one spot, bandannas in her long and straight hair, Barbarella boobs, Guess and Jordache jeans in every color of the palette, an army surplus bomber jacket, and those gray and purple Pegasus—the first Nikes you'd ever seen. She lived in an oceanfront two-story castle with a pool no one ever bathed in and a Spanish-speaking Chihuahua. Came to school in a black Targa, AC on rainy season to rainy season, driver in cutoffs and Wayfarers, jam of the day on loop. Knew the rock, the pop, the lock, the smurf, the wop. Fresher than fresh. Maybe, like you, a bit too far out for that little town. And her dad, too: a shadowy figure who some said dealt in weapons and mercenaries and drugs and all kinds of evil things. You've heard the rumors, you're eager to dispel or confirm. "Is is true," you ask, "that he's CIA?"

"No," Sabine laughs. "He's into import-export. But he does go to to Eastern Europe a lot. He has a plane, an Antonov, and his own airstrip in the bush."

The best thing about him is that he's never home. Of Sabine's mom, just a few words, and glamorous pictures. She was a Russian model who traveled the world and made good money before raising a family. She never took to Africa. She left after Sabine's brother wandered into the pole and drowned. They found her floating in the Danube.

So there's enough sadness there to fill the entire universe. So her father is restless and always gone. So Sabine has everything she could possibly want, but she is always alone, and she sips cranberry Nemiroff.

Over time Sabine forced you out of your shell. Bold, uncharted moonshots that went straight to your head and handily beat the most air you'd ever caught off a half-pipe, leaving no time for answers—only big, and ever bigger, questions. Asked you out only to stand you up. Jumped on your board and kissed you first. Flashed you on her balcony. Wore her Catholic School uniform with no bra and her miniskirts no panties. Gave you a taste in gym class. Stashed anagrams of your combined initials on her body's secret places. Loved you everywhere in that house—guava tree, shower, carpet, sofa, Targa, terrace. Everything you know about neediness, Neruda,

Prince, Woody Allen, Rick James, Lendl-McEnroe, Freud, Camus, Couture, and Space Invaders, she taught you. Romantics, shapeshifters, daydreamers, misfits planet-hopping hand in hand. Omnivores with eyes shut tight, a stubborn case of butterflies and an affinity for flight.

Sex wasn't sex, at first. It was everything but. It was making love. It was taking your time. It was yearning. It was learning. It was meaning. It was discovery. It was anticipation. It was entrusting each other with your most sacred possession. It was setting your bond in stone, choosing your camp, throwing in your lot, taking a chance on that person, looking into their eyes, saying their name, grabbing their hand, leaping together on a speeding train, leaving town with no map, no destination. It was adventure. It was living life.

You're ready, you're almost grown, you're full of yourself, and, outwardly, you're so so sure. You want this. You want each other. Time to take it further. This is for real. Tonight is the night. Just the two of you, intimacy a soundproof world-proof autonomous biome. Inner joy and contentment. Uncertainty a huge part of the deal, comes with the territory. Hoping, above all, that you won't disappoint. Will I know what to do? Will I be enough? What if I mess this up?

You read and you talk among boys and you catch glimpses of stuff in magazines or anatomy class or adult movies and you dig deeper but nothing prepares you, not really, no one shows you what to do. Everybody acts older than their age, everybody is experienced, everybody shows off, everybody mouths off, everybody pretends, no rookies among us, no trainees here, only champions, the crème de la crème, the cream of the crop, we're all studs, we're all jocks, we're all porn stars, we're all super endowed, we're all cold-hearted, we don't fall in love, we don't do foreplay, we get it up, we don't go down for nothing, we get right down to it, we go the distance, we run the gamut, we're marathon men, we give it good, we shoot and reload, we last all night.

So all this begs on your end for a little preparation, right? Some sort of figuring out. Like, first of all, what kind of man are you gonna be? It's one thing to skew quiet, moody, brooding, reserved, borderline shy. It's OK to be a loner, to shroud yourself in mystery, to move to your own beat, to pursue what you pursue. But what, exactly, is masculinity? Is it round-the-clock posturing, ironclad attitude, inexhaustible strength, head-to-toe self-control? Is it manipulation, total domination? Is it the permanent projection of a tough-guy, emotionless, no-fucks, never-cry, been-around-the-block, give-no-inch image? Is it keeping secrets and its predictable corollary, infidelity? Is it feelings, sensitivity, sharing, communication, vulnerability, gentleness, kindness, openness, transparency, honesty, goofiness, laughter, glee? You've heard all the horror stories. Boys marked for life for being too soft or too eager, boys tagged as the worst weaklings for not handling their business, for failing to raise the flag and get the job done at clarion call. How much frankness about your insecurities gets you propelled atop the pussies heap? Do you play-act? Do you put on a show? Do you believe the stories or do you become the best boyfriend you can be?

So you remind yourself to bring protection, to be good, to listen, to make her smile, to speak from the heart, to give your everything, to aim to please, to put in work, to demand nothing, to pay attention. Then you hold her. You find the words. You set them to music. You let her know she's beautiful. You describe how looking at her makes you feel inside. You tell her she's a world unto herself. You tell her Rigel, the prettiest star in Orion, pales in comparison. You promise you'll take care of her. You tell her she makes you better, spirited and so so free, boundless energy, impetus unleashed. You tell her kissing her is just like floating in the dark: same awesome peace, silver and blue and black, everything quiet, no more doubt, her heartbeat your soundtrack. Being together feels that right, it's the ultimate truth, the kind of knowledge they don't teach in class—you're where you're meant to be, your search over before it begins, you've lucked out, you've already found the one.

And eventually, that special moment, your first time, your supernova, you kind of get it right. It sings happiness, it glows, it flows, it bursts with sensation, it lives on and on and on, it is one in a million, it is filled with tenderness, slowness, sweetness, calm, new perceptions, a little momentousness. Pleasure and physical fulfillment, not so much, not in the middle of the act itself. "I was in pain," she will admit many years later. "I was everywhere but in that room. Everywhere but on that bed. What you call

9

'dissociation.' It hurt real real bad. I couldn't wait for you to stop. I prayed for it to end."

And so it remains, in your memory, the greatest gift Sabine would ever bestow.

You thought it would last forever. You wanted it to. There was nothing like it. No one had this, as far as you knew. But sometimes, in space's mesmerizing emptiness and blue ink night, your wings would give out, you would run out of breath and blame your oxygen supply. Sometimes, marveling at poignant and fragile Earth, you would wonder if love is all there is to life. Sometimes you would get restless and crash, couldn't get back. What kind of knowledge was out there, waiting to be uncovered? Was there a way to exist in the middle? All you knew was super-high highs. Days shrunken into what you could fit in with Sabine. Would it hurt, you wondered, to wander, check out for a while? You missed being alone. You missed you. That secluded beach of yours where the Atlantic comes to slam against a wall of jagged cliffs with exhilarating fury, splashing you with mist, freeing your spirit whenever you feel raw or stuck or just plain low—bet you could drop the bird nearby, slow things down a notch, regroup and recenter, knock on wood, kick it just to kick it, skip a rock or two, sit around. Become a wave, a force of your own, the ocean that rears its many heads and roars. So, without putting it in so many words, you eased on the throttle, keyed in new coordinates, switched to landing altitude. It would all be there, you figured, should you reconsider. You were 17, by then. 17 and a burned-out outlier.

11

"You're leaving, Surfer?" You nod and grab your deck. They sneak up on you, jack you up, pull you opposite ways: personal quest; precocious regret.

"There's this new Plateau spot. Fresh pavement. Nice and smooth. Can't wait to get out there. See what I can do." She takes her Anaïs, Ysatis, Shalimar, Opium, Poison, and Coco, flings them one after the other across the room, hitting the wall and the mirror, shattering a window inches from you. Fight or Flight? Pain wins, and not for the last time. You put your board down, sit on it, bury your head, disappear, teleport out. *Broken glass / Everywhere*. Same old story, as you can see—the people close to you are also the ones who're going to harm you. Violence again having its way, seizing you up, shutting you down, reeling you in. *This is what it sounds like / When doves cry.*

The whole time, you thought it was you. Can't say you didn't have issues. But Sabine was crazy, too. Nature, Nurture, maybe a little touch of the two. Kept trying to try again after you split up for the hundredth time because nothing else was working for her. Not the film school classmate whose dad was some sort of Truffaut. Not the coyote from Tijuana who mistook her for Parry Hearst. Not the Algerian boxer who suffered one too many blows to the head and did his best to drive her to suicide, de Sade to her Justine—a sadist will do what a sadist does. Finally found what you've been looking for, you mused from your frigid cell in the Archipelago; and it brought you no peace, no satisfaction. So from here, my dear, where do you go?

You'd seen that side of her, of course. The side that craved pain and kept asking. Mickey Rourke-Kim Basinger, *9 1/2 Weeks*, her hand in your crotch the whole time. *L'Amant*, Marguerite Duras. *L'Histoire d'Adèle H*, Adjani. Was it you who awakened the monster, broke Sabine in? Junior year, your birthday fell on a Sunday. Inside her bedroom, guava jelly on her body, cake all over the sheets, Lord knows you didn't mean to, blame it on *Give It to Me Baby*, blame it on *Lady Cab Driver*, blame it on the candles, blame it on *Blame It on the Boogie:* in the heat of it you slipped and slid and smashed and smushed and went in the way you shouldn't have been. "Feels … so … good…." she moaned, in the throes of something dark, something new, scooting the better to feel you, biting, thrashing, quivering, rising from under you. That, right there, was your line. That was your clue.

Enter the Dragon. Spooked, unsure, you chilled and hung back, leaned toward waiting out the gathering monsoon, monitored windsocks and weather balloons for air currents, atmospheric pressure and temperature. But Sabine knew just what she was onto. "I want to be hurt," she confessed, looking you in the eye, freeze-drying something inside of you, and you took it all the way far, you threw it out of bounds, you took it to 100, you extrapolated, you heard belted, choked, spanked, slapped, struck, called a bitch, called a slut, pimped, punished, blindfolded, tied, humiliated, debased, dumped.

You were too immature to realize it, but it took guts, and a whole lot of trust, for Sabine to reveal herself. That being said, how was watching other dudes do her supposed to do something for you? "Pain is pleasure," she ventured, never one to give up, dropping hints here and there, Quasar-5 feelers spinning past your Alpha Centauri hangout untethered unwelcome and unanswered, Sista Sabine on that Book of Explorations roller coaster, All in attendance please turn to line 15, page 500. "I want you to stand by the bed and light a cigarette. I'll be on my stomach, looking into your eyes the whole time. It just can't be anyone from our school." Oh, the things Sabine itched to get into.

For a couple of years, those words hung between the two of you. You tried to understand. She tried to entice you. It cheapened her, made you think less of her. It girl to old standby. In the end, you simply didn't have it in you. No sorcerer's apprentice, no playing with fire, no yes-ma'am voodoo. Did you, that young, that early, foresee the guilt either choice could and would pop on you? Mr. No, she took to calling you. Mr. No Good. Mr. No Fun. Mr. Nogoodfun. All you felt was pity, fear, confusion. You weren't ready to let go of your innocence, or maybe innocence wasn't ready to let go of you. Where, the reset button? Where, the escape pod? Where, the trail out of the woods? *All I want is some peace of mind / With a little love I'm tryin' to find.*

"Stay with me," she pleaded. "Stay." Were you doomed because you wouldn't, couldn't give her that stuff she coveted?

She is Apollonia in the backdoor's half light. Evening gloves, garter belt, houri eyeshadow, lace décolleté, strawberry lips. Game but a little unsure, a touch tentative. *Tonight I'm living in a fantasy / Do you think I'm a nasty girl?* "Tell me," she whispers, kisses soft and burning-hot and sensuously slow, hair in her face, flames rising in the wake of circles and lines

15

and arabesques like gasoline to a geisha's match, graffitis on your body, tattoo in every little touch, sighs and goosebumps and starlight and fireflies and the satisfaction of shared emotion and the stillness of time as she sketches and draws and fills in the color and nibbles and hums, *Je suis l'as de trèfle / Qui pique ton coeur*. "Tell me what you want me to do. Tell me who you want me to be." Those blood-red stilettos both intrigue and excite you. That one scene in Kundera's book, when a woman undresses and stands above a mirror hands on hips and legs apart, has always stuck with you. Do boots, you wonder, puncture as they walk all over you?

You more or less autopiloted to the exosphere. Suited up, morphed into your highest incarnation: demigod status ± the complications. Discovered it is both a rush and a minefield to be adored without reservations. What good, idols that won't deliver? *Sorrow's in our hearts / And our spirits are broken / But don't stop / Being kind to one another.*

Regime changes swift, bewildering, brutal: Toppled overnight, sentenced without due process, exiled to some hellish forced-labor gulag. Solitary confinement for fighting and foul mouth. Rules, Rehabilitation, peepholes, barbed wire, metal doors, cold, coal pits, frostbite, -40C padded face masks, the beguiling spruce trees of the taiga, one single sorry step past the miradors' line of sight and they shoot you, beat you senseless, leave you outside naked if they catch you, leave it to exposure to dispatch you. 200 daily grams of bread, gnat porridge, roach soup, raw potatoes, no fire, no knife, dip them in the snow, take a bite. Soul sustenance is

Radio Free free-form jazz and reverse-propaganda programs that all say, Hold on, the thaw is coming, the thaw is on its way, the thaw is coming on. Among your fellow prisoners, no true revolutionaries that you can see. They superfluously ask, "What are you in for?" and your shrugged-off tossed-off repartee, "For Love," it never varies, and then they invariably add, with a sly profile and an ounce of sadness and the glint of recognition and shallow breath and rotten scurvy teeth and the remnants of a broken spirit, "So are we." You have two pet mice, one you name Proud, the other Angry. You wish for one more, maverick little Stealthy, for kamikaze missions to the shoddy commissary. Day 140, word is out: The replacement is definitely not working out, the replacement is on his way out. You're on high alert, looking out for the black Targa's frog eyes and low growl, throw balloon tires on that bitch and straight above marshes and ponds and peat bogs and Stalin's abandoned train tracks she'll hovercraft. Sure enough, Wayfarers at the gate with flip-top boxes of Smooth Rich Mellow Mellow for your habit, gift-wrapped Kouros because *Les dieux vivants ont leur parfum*, translucent 76 mm Kryptonics for speed, warm Poilâne and guava jelly for old times' sake. Official apology. Reinstatement papers on lavender Party stationary. Tearful, grateful, triumphant return, There once was a princess who lived in a castle by the sea. Sabine's lips, Sabine's touch, Sabine's flawless legs squeezing you in the tub—*Pretty Woman*. Your soul brimming with helium once more, eagle among eagles, I Survived Camp Siberia sweatshirt. *Your love is a / House for I.*

17

Was Sabine your servant or your master? Mephistopheles what, Mephistopheles who? You only wanted the sweet tender moments. Downhill Corniche wind just like cool Cali kids. She laughs and tries to hold the hibiscus in her hair. You curse because you can't see, she's moving so much and you're going too fast. Not one cloud in the warm friendly lovers' sky. She sits on the handlebars and shines. Electric-blue bodysuit and pink leg warmers, feet on the front pegs, back so snug on your chest your cheeks touch. You steady the ride, find your groove and then you glide. Happy, invincible, unstoppable. You're forever young, she's forever yours—if they try and tell you any different you'll punch them where it hurts.

Endless talks, the vibe, beach house romps, sunset walks. Lagon II pontoon dinners, the culture, the country, the future. You call her "Chabine," not because she's from the French West Indies, but because it rhymes, because of her freckles and complexion.

Her old man, henchman on a mission, is never home for a reason: Ethiopia, Somalia, Tchad, Niger, Sudan, Ciskei, Transkei, Zaïre, Liberia, Uganda, Rwanda, Burundi … he's in and out of every hot spot, he's in much demand, he does his best to supply it all: machine guns, ammunition, grenades, uniforms, boots, MREs, RPGs, satellite phones…. Whatever fits inside the Antonov's belly, down to jeeps and tanks and cannons. That is what he imports and exports, the ghetto kid from Katanga who made it to a desk at the Union Minière before finding his way to Ukraine and becoming the sinews of war, aka Mr. Bad News.

She adores him. He's all she has. But he's restless, he's always gone, he's up to no good, and she's left with nothing but memories and Nutella crepes and Nemiroff inside her decked-out palatial home. He takes pictures and videos from battlefield fringes and he shares his wonderment for flying geese formations, the bend of windswept grass on a red hill, the deadly calm of a gas-spewing lake. A few years in, the tapes and pictures bore and tire her. She resents his lifestyle, the dives he dips in, the whores he cavorts with. "I can't stand to be in that house," he says. "I can't bear looking at that fucking pool."
She says, "How do you think I feel? Why don't we fucking move?"

She gives you hell for the cigarettes you so carelessly chain-smoke since middle school. She snatches them, she breaks them, she throws them out. You go and buy 10- or 20-packs, you buy from street hacks by the stick. Everywhere you turn in your city, Bob Norris plays Pied Piper to you and each and every Francophonie kid. Iconic macho posters above rooftop clotheslines and the cinderblock skyline. Ubiquitous radio ads, "*Jelël me meyla bène Marlboro*" to *Magnificent Seven* harmonica overtures. Intimations of roving tumbleweeds, bucking broncos, bareback rodeos; dark-skinned cowboys striking up and lighting up by campfires; cattle at rest; piping-hot coffee in chipped tin mugs; ladles half-immersed in simmering pork and beans. It's pushy. It's cringy. It's condescendingly creepy. You laugh about it together, you miss the point: Against this marketing blitz you do not stay a single chance. It will take you years to rid yourself of your tobacco addiction.

Like all teenagers, you're gloomy about your future. Sabine, not so much. Like you, she's already seen her share of bad in the world. Unlike you, she does her best to shrug it off. Nutella, Nemiroff, overseas shopping sprees, Kalashnikov heiress with an allowance triple the yearly salary, hopscotches across the footprint cutouts of the gold-plated rainbow all the way to her straight-shot destiny. And it is all so very complicated and insidious and surreal —how you've become so close to her in such a short time; the nicotine, the cool factor, flirting with cancer; the perks, the gifts, the lifestyle, the luxury dwellings; the guards, the chauffeurs, the cars; eating at the Don's table in the midst of Third World misery. Should her father's sins be Sabine's to carry? By cavorting and associating, are you equally guilty?

You don't believe in the rat race, in profiting at all cost, in Me first, in the Winner takes all philosophy. You're a die-hard Trotskyist. The Don is anything but a fool, he senses something, he's not as immune to judgement as he seems, corroding thick skin, shield ripping at the seams. Maybe he's only sharing a few tips, prepping you for succession or leadership, an "I did it my way" kind of thing. In your one good conversation, the Don tells you it's easy, as a teen, to show compunction, to wear ambivalence on your sleeve, to try on different avatars, to have a conscience, to Bermuda Triangle gray zones, to pledge decency. "Where I'm from you think on your feet, you bark and you bite, you eat what you kill. I had to survive on my own. I had to fight and push and claw and elbow my way out of the basket of crabs, you best believe. No one spotted me. Let's see, when you're out there with your back against the wall, if idealism is an option still."

The one thing you retain from this one-sided exchange is how banal evil looks. You'd never think, by looking at the man, that he is who he is and does what he does. He's already lost his hair; the most he manages to grow is a sorry excuse of a beard; he wears glasses; his cargoes hang under his belly. Sabine, who takes after her model mom, is already taller than him. He never departs from a studied calm. Violence, you realize, can assume many forms.

You wish you could see the Antonov. Niet, says the Don. He's learned, over time, to separate business from family. You give it a good shrug and focus on Sabine, you do your best to forget the old man and his dirty deeds.

Sabine. Didn't she, when your parents blasted you for talking of becoming a writer, staunchly root for you? Capote, she called you. Camelot, too. "In old Senghor's mansion at the bottom of the Boulevard we'll raise flamingos, entertain pop stars, host heads of state and convert the Pope. You'll fix whatever's the matter with the eight regions and the city. I'll bake lemon meringues, slink past security in a skintight studded shameless strapless sparky tiny little thingy and sultrily sing 'Happy Birthday to you, *chéri*' on National TV." Sabine was your woman, friend, muse, teacher, emblem, impresario, figurehead, religion, advocate, pompom girl, magnetic field, on-again off-again love. Couldn't have cared less about that kinky business. It was plain to see you'd get over the hump and get married someday, have a baby and call him Nate (if it was a boy), start a family.

She, too, had her doubts. The push-pull, the elephant in the room, reunions bleeding into reruns, separations like aborted missions, scenarios like *Le Dernier Tango*. There were places she went where you couldn't reach her. Parts of her would never belong to you. Parts of you would never belong to her. You had fought for your own right to disconnect here and there, those sabbatical days or weeks or months when "space" actually meant physical, if never emotional, separation, a little distance, time apart, a circle of one.

If only you'd gotten a dollar for each time one of you quit and came back, quit and came back, quit and came back. "Trust me," you said. "Trust me, and never forget." That small sentence became her mantra and your motto. You looked on as she had it engraved on the back of her Bulgari, somewhere on glittering Rue de la Paix, amazed that words could have such resonance, hoping their power would be enough. Guess you were the best she'd ever had, measure for measure, all things considered—her first love. Popped that cherry, didn't you? All that time, too much time, alone in her big empty fortress—there are no adults in your story. *Kama Sutra*, movies, literature, music, chocolate, muesli, truffles, the best couches, blinds always half drawn, the micro dog calling you *pendejo* out of sheer jealousy, everything purple. You called it *Situation #9*. A passion so intoxicating it nearly mushroomed you. Your entire teenage years spent with the first girl you ever spoke to?

Dawo wôto senlatâ—Alone, a bangle does not jingle.

But it all got old, see? It all went dead cold. You had to fight off sleep with everything in you after swearing it was over for the last time because you were at the end of your rope and she was off her lithium—she'd graduated from cranberry Nemiroff to medical-grade stuff. "I know what I have to do," she told you. Eyes dry as last July, she who cried for any- and everything—the ozone layer, stranded whales, children begging at traffic lights, *Casablanca*, *The Purple Rose of Cairo*, Solzhenitsyn, Yasser Arafat,

Soweto. No tone, no inflection, real flat, cold-blooded, absentminded-like, looking at the wall in her striped pajamas and Tex Avery tee—even then, those sanctified boobs were calling thee. "Kill you, and then kill me." And you thought, *Sometimes it snows in April / Sometimes I feel so bad.* So you took her meds out of her purse, hid all the knives but forgot the scissors, and tried hard to stay awake, only to come to and see her staring dead at you at 7 in the a.m., same empty emotionless damn near catatonic gaze—*37.2 Le Matin*. Fallen angel what, fallen angel who? TALM (This Ain't Lake Minnetonka).

That was Sabine. What happened with Anaëlle was lemongrass friendship that bloomed and bloomed and became something more and something new. You exited a dry spell and happened upon a splash of green sweeping the heartrending vista. A balm, the seed of eternal life, the gift of water, the miracle of light. A traveler's refuge, a pilgrim's paradise, a hermit's temptation, a settler's dream, an oasis lush enough for two. Chattering ostriches and playful cheetahs defectors from Noah's Ark. The shade of arcing trees. Roots like offshoots seeking the molten core of Mother Earth. Dates soft succulent nutrient, the kiss of sugar. You did love Anaëlle, and you did care. Just not enough to try and figure out what it was that was missing. Just not enough to walk back the hand of time, reverse-cross the sea and snatch her away from whoever. Trapped inside Pac-Man, ghosts of moments past hot on your trail, new corridors every day. You could have screamed: *Let's get back to love!* You could have begged: *Bring it all back to me / Where it's supposed to be*. You didn't feel the need, the strength, the hurry. Your oasis but a momentary respite, temporary rescue, parking garage, short-term storage for your rambling heart. *When our time is ended / How will we have spent it?*

Enter the Dragon. Your own brand of darkness had started manifesting itself—side kicks, choke holds, Supreme® nunchucks, punches that stunned your infinite reflections in the Hall of Mirrors and ragdolled you across the blue dojo floor. Shit. The taste of blood when you brought your fingers to your lips. Damn. You had completely lost your way, slow-mo lagging, kata glitchy, Tao inferior. Your wretched childhood on the other line, the pitch suddenly impossible to ignore, drowning out the main event. From a jock to a bum. From a hum to a scream. From color to black and white. Everything stale. Everything blah. Like a leave of absence from your own life. Like watching it all unfold from the bleachers in the fog of CTE with a heart in dry season and an empty smile and a body slowly shutting down. You were *desafinado*—out of tune.

"I need to see a shrink," you told Papa as a last resort, overcome with sadness once more. "That is not us," Papa said calmly. "That is not who we are. That is not what we do."

What we do is take you to marabout after marabout. Seers, holy men, shamans whose opaqueness stinks of sleight of hand and knowledge of sacred texts vaunted to heal all afflictions past, present or future. What we do is cling to the belief that our own existence is beyond our comprehension, that we are powerless in shaping it, that we have no control over our destiny, that happiness, safety, health, work, education, material comfort, relationships, procreation, status, and, eventually, spiritual salvation, will not, cannot be obtained or maintained without continually assuaging a pantheon of jinns conducting business through aloof, unvetted, self-appointed, self-accredited middlemen.

What we do is sit in dark cluttered spaces listening to unintelligible mutterings and invocations, surrendering our intelligence, agency, autonomy, strength, and sense of rationality. What we do is smash eggs on baobab trunks; bury wishes inside knots of rough cloth; wear silver to thwart envy and jealousy; pin gris-gris to the inside of our clothing; drink magic potions that taste of hydromel; splash on the strongest Sandaga patchouli to mask the rotten decoctions of roots and leaves and twigs we must bathe in for protection; slather on snake oil for good luck; and draw in the sand secret symbols for a safe return before stepping outside our door each morning.

What we do is sacrifice sheep and cattle and poultry and hypocritically call it alms for the poorest of the poor.

What we do is throw money to the wind and wood into the pyre of superstition well over a half-century after Indépendance. What we do is perpetuate the parallel universe of teachings and practices that rushed into the void left by colonization, the annihilation of our peoples' cultures and ways of life, the collapse of our social structures and belief systems. What we do is hold on to paganism and sorcery and witchcraft disguised as benign ancient traditions. What we do is remain enthralled to charlatans and con men who become privy to our secrets, provide a conduit for our basest instincts, enable the worst in our character.

What we do is take an ill-afforded detour in our quest for a viable way between wholesale embrace of Eurocentric values and our ancestors' mode of relating to the Universe. The White man came and the White man left, more or less. We are not who we were. We don't know how to be. This realm we now inhabit isn't the one we created for ourselves. It is the one imposed upon us, the one we are still trying to adapt to, with aims and methods as varied as we are, and degrees of success to boot. What does it mean to be West African in the late 20th Century? *This is the age of reality / But some of we deal with mythology / This is the age of science and technology / But some of we check for Antiquity.*

Papa had gone from barefoot street soccer legend in a sun-scorched peanut town to Lycée Van Vollenhoven in the capital, and then on to *Agrégation* in Paris, returning with his young family to a fifteen-year-old nation hungry for talent. He began teaching and simultaneously joined the Ministry of Public Health, where he quickly rose to the number two slot: Director of Pharmacy. Built the legal framework and infrastructure through which medicine could be tested, vetted, imported, distributed, bought, sold, and, eventually, produced. Oversaw the supply pipeline to Le Dantec, nicknamed "Poor man's hospital," West Africa's only large-scale facility dedicated to treating people of color. Crisscrossed the countryside in a Volkswagen Type 181 to set up a network of state-run clinics and dispensaries. He would be gone for long stretches at a time, bringing back wicker baskets containing more fruit and produce than the family could possibly consume: sugarcane from the northwestern plains where the river that shares the country's name runs into the sea; yellow-skinned *agrumes* from the mangroves of the secession-prone South; watermelons that were dark-green, perfectly round, bright-red on the inside; *konis* whose juice stained your shirts and flesh was softer than a coconut's; *guertés* — peanuts eaten fresh off the ground, boiled in the shell, or roasted in sand; *mbokh* — ears of corn that were slow-grilled on a bed of embers, their popped kernels a special treat;

bouye, from the baobab tree, which, with generous spoonfuls of peanut butter and a bit of milk, became delicious *ngalakh* smoothie; the mostly tart variety of jujubes called *sideem*; the succulent *madda*, an oversized pod with a thick and rugged outer layer, edible inner skin, seeds that turned fleshy and syrupy with just the right blend of water, sugar, salt, pepper, and Arome Maggi; *corosol*, the pulp of which Maman whipped and froze into ice cream; *sapoti*, furry and oval as a kiwi, only sweeter; *oul*, the powder of which could be compacted into purplish square cakes; *ditakh*, flat and fiber-rich, whose pigment colored your fingers, lips, and teeth emerald-green.

Whether to the interior or conferences in other countries, Papa seemed to always be away, leaving to Maman most of the household and child-rearing responsibilities. She was also a pioneer in her own way. An educated, professionally employed mother of four who loved music and the arts. A Classic beauty whose looks came with a deep well of love, an iron will and an infallible sense of style—Saint Laurent at the *méchoui* receptions she gave on your front lawn; regal, sumptuously embroidered boubous for Saint-Michel autumn strolls.

They both remained firmly rooted in their African-ness, which may or may not explain the marabouts. Could be the talismans he periodically found hidden away in his office drawers or taped under his desk chair, prompting him to thoroughly sweep the place after each return: indecipherable inscriptions folded inside leather pouches; tiny horns that contained strange mixtures of powder, bark, and soil; or yet more baffling glyphs and drawings. Maman accidentally disinterred such otherworldly objects while gardening or repotting. Sometimes they hung from your fig or Malabar almond trees like cocoons awaiting metamorphosis. If nothing else, they reeked of malefice and evil intent.

Those discoveries became frequent enough and unsettling enough to induce a pervasive feeling of paranoia in your parents over the years. They, like the mysterious deaths of your beloved German shepherds, and every misfortune that happened to beset the family, were the work of "enemies"; people, most likely within the government, who wanted Papa demoted, sacked, divorced, ruined, finished, his children incapacitated by malady, failing school, their future gone. What were Papa and Maman to do in order to save themselves, protect their own? Fire must be fought with fire. They, too, started seeking out savants versed in the occult sciences, genies' underlings able to offer counter weapons to the weapons they had no understanding of.

That door, once opened, was never closed. It became the lens through which most of your lives was explained and understood. Adversaries. Attacks. Spells. Defense. Preemptive strikes. It was all but impossible, as a child, not to feel confused. How could someone who had managed to become the first Black man to obtain a doctorate in his field still believe in spirits? How to fight, and win, a war against unseen adversaries who delved in the supernatural—if supernatural was indeed a thing?

You went along out of respect for your folks and because of your customary sense of duty, having long ago lost the war of opinions. Nothing you said or did was going to change Papa and Maman's minds. Marabouts had always been their way of caring for you. Who were you to deny them those gestures of affection, those manifestations of deep concern? Did it matter what and who they believed in? This was a fight for another day.

More than ever before, you were left to your own devices. Over the course of several months, you retreated within and started sealing all the hatches. No one in, no one out. Going down down down. The Atlantic now immobile and dense and cold and devoid of life like the cosmos, like the Sahel that looms and grows, desert that never ebbs, only flows. Sought neither companionship nor certainty; the other end of the rainbow, aloneness and randomness, just as unbearable. So you lurked inside in-between lands, citizen of no nation, at once nowhere and everywhere, too disoriented to be aware, inappreciative of your blessings when they finally came. Flux, movement, newness, danger, adventure, life in a whole new galaxy, yes. Out West. Out there. Far from that place that didn't begin to understand you, had nothing to offer the likes of you. As a fresh beginning, a jumpstart out of the numbness, a frigid-water swim, a shock to the system, a reboot, an end to the paralysis. Anaëlle wasn't any of those things. Not an unexplored planet, not a continent, not a country, not even a neon-flooded city. Just a rock-solid, well-grounded, easygoing, honest, smart, thoughtful, earnest, beautiful girl. It couldn't have worked. The missing piece was you. You were stuck in place, running on empty, running for your life, looking for the next rocket launch out. You're the one who got away.

She's the one who stayed. Went to Polytechnique Thiès, became an economist in less time than it took you to find your bearings, get accustomed to the winters, perfect your English, anoint "biatch" your favorite word. Joined a string of N.G.O.s bringing relief to the drought-stricken Northeast—pretty textbook, straightforward stuff: food banks; health clinics; micro loans to enterprising young girls and mothers; irrigation pumps, seeds and fertilizer for farmers. Each project she sees through meticulously but perfunctorily, aware that the solution lies elsewhere, because we all must start somewhere, because you gotta crawl before you walk, because this is no one size fits all, because the payoff is in the empirical: seeing and learning these far-flung regions and their isolated, sunbaked, forgotten hamlets for herself. Thousands of rutted kilometers in a secondhand stick shift Pajero. Red-earth tracks stretching toward the horizon long after the pavement and utility grid. Trees and shrubbery intermittent. Wild animal sightings nonexistent, Noah's Ark what, Noah's Ark who? Heat, dust, stifling Harmattan air. Grasshoppers flying into the windshield and through the open windows. She sings along to the mixtapes you made her. Hiking boots, sunglasses, a scarf in muted tones because women must show modesty and cover their hair in the places she goes. Laptop, sunblock, First-Aid, mosquito relief, army surplus backpack. Shared meals with families inside huts humbling in their simplicity, for lack of a better description; communal bowl of red rice and the cheapest of fish into which the sand also finds its way; aluminum silverware unpacked ceremoniously; colorful water goblets of scratched plastic from a clay *canari*; straw mat covering the moldy dirt floor; toys cobbled from tomato paste cans, pieces of string and strands of cloth that Warhol wouldn't have disowned.

The strengthening grip of the desert witnessed firsthand. Flies at the corner of toddlers' mouths. Newborn deaths. Distended bellies. One-room schools. Idle young adults. Empty wells. Skeletal herds. Parched and barren fields. This is what she came to see; what she will take back with her; what motivates her always. "We are tired," they tell her village after village, usually after the ice has been broken and business taken care of. Long after dusk, resignation rising with the pale yellow moon. Enamel tea kettle bubbling over a small fire. Kora instrumentals on the radio turned down low. Kola split in half and chewed slowly. The ever-present peanuts. Smiles and pleasantries and thank-yous giving way to the weariness that is so at home here that it pervades everything: atmosphere; outlook; movement; speech cadence; the quality of the light. "We are tired."

Sometimes what she has to offer is far from meeting the need. Sometimes the little she brings is big enough to stoke envy, jealousy, cupidity, the insecurities of traditional chiefs, the unease of elders, the restlessness of husbands. For people who truly have nothing, the littlest thing is something. She must quickly assess situations, judge character, identify allies, ward off bullies, appoint stewards, tiptoe around sensibilities or crush them. "I'm not always the bearer of good news. If only I could just drop the stuff off, get it working, and leave. There are a million other things to worry about. The human element."

Money is tight. She scrimped and managed to put something down on a tiny house in an overcrowded neighborhood called Liberté, baptized it Racines. Wishful thinking, you say, sounding hollow to your own ears.

And yet. Unrest is spreading in your hometown. Rioting youths periodically overturn cars and set shops ablaze, clash with gendarmes from behind barricades. Stones and Molotov straight out of Mai '68.

The whole country, according to you, is a powder keg. Ecology like *Mercy Mercy Me*; corruption as entrenched as ever; all land of value grabbed long ago by religious leaders, government officials, foreign entities; the coast all but depleted of marine life; tourism and industry incapable of providing the needed jobs; the time bomb of population growth; religious conservatism on the rise; the fear that, just like everywhere else around these parts, the army will someday spill out of rundown barracks and attempt a power grab.

Anaëlle remains undeterred. Tends her garden on Sundays and asks herself if she's making enough of an impact. Her next move never far from her thoughts: PhD, public service, private sector, World Bank, F.A.O.? What is clear is that nothing is going to stop her. Call her talented. Call her inspired. Call her expert. Call her powerful. Call her idealistic. Call her the Future.

So all our young need not leave in order to achieve. Anaëlle is living proof: Africa does not eat its own.

It is hard not to see a rebuttal in her choice. So you question yourself: Do I love where I'm from? Does it love me? Was it the place itself or just the mentality? Are they inseparable? Would I also have thrived, had I stayed? Will I ever return?

"I still read your poems," she tells you. "I think they're beautiful."

You need wisdom and rescuing, too. Who does she share her breakthrough ideas about cheap cellphones, reforestation, solar panels and free internet with? Who does she call to unwind after a long day at the office or trip in the bush? Soon you start losing touch and it's no longer you.

Maybe this is why in all your dreams of Anaëlle she wears white and heels, hair brushed all the way out, comes in peace, brings you comfort, and you run to her. And that smile makes you warm all over. And those dreams have you tossing, turning, crooning: *If you could only know my feelings / You would know how much / I do believe.* Why are some things just not meant to be? It's Anaëlle's kindness that you will miss the most. The fact that she, unlike E, unlike Sabine, was about you, and into you, good for you, and good to you. Life is casualties, collateral, complications, vagueness, gray zones, misunderstandings, missed connections, misconceptions, mourning, PONR (Point of No Return).

Drive me crazy
Drive me all night
Just don't break up
The connection

And then there was E. 17 to your 28, two kids, the projects. No degree, no prospects. Pops locked up, mama on dope since the '80s. Owned 14th Street. Eyes like a deviant Bambi, belly dances like Istanbul, the gravitational pull of 1,000 ancient suns. Laugh that sounded better than the Billboard Hot 100. Brown sugar all over her booga wooga. *You're much too much / Too much for one man / But not enough for two.* Everywhere you turned, dudes with names like Taz, Fonz, Smoke, D-Low, Bun Bun, Boo Boo—she liked them dark, street, strapped. *Who is he? / And what is he to you?* Much as you hate to say it, much as you abhor that word, she liked *niggas.* But never mind.

You tuned in to those government towers and picked up a distress beacon. Met children who never smiled, and thought, *Hollis Brown.* Claimed that S-logo cape, jumped into the souped-up coupe, floored it, and so on and so on. Years on the job, pedal to the metal, no holds barred, no belt on. Father to her sons. Icarus to her 1,000 suns. Crash-test dummy to

41

her affection. Misguided savior. Unrequited Pygmalion. You just kept keeping on.

Love is blindness / I don't want to see. You asked, and E wrapped the night so very tight around thee.

Your fault line her sweet spot. *Ooh, are you my baby / Or are we just friends?* Slave to her wants, antidote to the kids' needs. Classic case of Transfer: What you didn't get as a child is what you tried to give her. They forgot to tell you one small simple truth —well, make that two: First, your name wasn't Ta-Doow, you didn't own the motherfucker; second, it ain't no such thing as a Superman.

Out the coupe and red cape, in Don Quixote and Rocinante. You slammed into those towers with all your heart and no helmet. Sifted for vestiges of humanity, kindness, decency, a little innocence. The stakes had never been higher. *What a weepin' and a wailin' and a gnashing of teeth / When the wicked and the righteous mee*t. But where I and I suffer, Babylon makes the rules.

Her dancer's belly your favorite pillow. Not one stretch mark, which in itself is remarkable. She never bothered decorating the joint. You didn't, either. Not a single picture on the walls. Phone, cable TV, air conditioning, enough closet space for all her designer stuff and she was good to go.

She doesn't work. You're never here. She and her homegirls have the run of the place. Somebody always needs their hair done. You come home exhausted from doubles on your feet to a clueless teenage mom of two who fills her time with frills, thrills, and futility; kids who don't call you Daddy; gel jars and grease stains; the lingering smell of the curling iron; bottomless bags of dirty laundry; Chinese takeout downed standing in the mini kitchen; the fridge all but ravaged; dishes in the sink and dust on the stove; trash overflowing with chip bags, melted Slurpees, loaded diapers, discarded braids, weave strands, wig clippings, pizza crust, paper plates. Sometimes the girls are still here. Laughing, smoking, gossiping while you despair for a moment to yourself before bed. Can't find the headspace to lay down a single worthy line in your Moleskine lately. Kenny, the custodian, says the traffic is constant. "All day long, they come and go. Sometimes it be men, too."

Her mom and junkie auntie you welcome in the name of compassion. Learn CPR, look out for needles, keep Narcan sprays close. Three overdoses between the two of them. They are the true living dead, legends around these streets. Banned for life from corner stores and area malls. Substance abuse veterans, HIV/ AIDS poster children. Way beyond repair, holding on by a thread. Rehab repeat offenders, recovery never a serious long-term option —they'd just as soon take the methadone and run. Gaunt face, lost stare, crab walk. Matchstick limbs, ant jumps, pockmarks. Loose teeth, jaundice, joint pain, cramps, swelling, smells. E's loud and passé Juicy velours tracksuits. Tacky rings sliding off bony fingers, mind a windswept wasteland.

Walk in, perk up, zero in. Swipe your Chicago Ones, Doernbecher Sixes, Bred Fours, Fire Red Fives. Flip that ASAP, go pay the pusher, run right back. Get high in your bathroom, burn Kush sticks to cover their tracks. Nod off, zone out, crash on the couch. You plunge the stopped-up toilet, a plethora of empty crack bags reaches back. Swirling around the bowl, they trumpet their sordid tale. And you recoil. And you stiffen. And you stifle a yowl.

The closest thing you have to a friend is Abdul. Wears a kufi and long black robes, sets up shop on the sidewalk right in front of your job. You've argued many times about the Nation and Sunni Islam, Farrakhan and Malcolm's assassination, conspiracy theories, the bootleg music he peddles by the trunkful that you staunchly refuse to touch—"Artists gotta get paid for every CD and cassette, my dude! That's how we make a living." He offers you the latest *Final Call*; bean pies; straight, no-bull advice: "I seen them kicks fly past. Sure did. I been known them crackhead ladies. Had a feeling that shit was yours. Wouldna copped regardless on account it was so hot. Deadstock vintage Js but no box?" Shakes his head, goes back to brushing his beard, looks straight into your eyes. "Been around long enough to know a good brother when I see one. If nothin' else, my bids in the Feds taught me that. That little red girl will never know you're the best thing that coulda happen to her. This here ain't no place to be real, Habibi. No country for a Black man. You bound to lose your soul. Hard as you work? I was you? Pack what's left of my stuff and run fast as I can. Get the hell on out somewhere. Back to the motherfuckin' Motherland."

You gaze out of your apartment window and see only chasm and distance and fracture—*They come / They come / To build a wall between us*. "You didn't tell me you were seeing other people."

"That's because you never asked."

This is what it means to be together and apart at the same time. To be fully into someone and completely, devastatingly alone. The one lesson you learned so very early, way too early, still holding strong: The people close to you are the ones who harm you. But will you ever, for God's sake, understand when it's time to let go, know where you do and don't belong?

E.T. phone home. You didn't seek out pain and humiliation. You derived no joy from being mistreated. You just showed too high a threshold, an inordinate ability to endure and absorb. You were no masochist. You weren't weak. What you were was a *sufferah*.

"I have to keep going for the boys," is what you told your family. "They look up to me. They truly have nobody."

"Come back," Maman implored you in response. "Come home."

"*Yidde ko yida dum, ko sammude sawavere*," Papa mused—To love one who doesn't love you is like culling morning dew from trees.

But that, of course, was the last thing you wanted to hear.

You barely made it out alive. Clocked shift after shift, zero days off, gauges maxed out across the dash. Needle jumping and jumping, Bonneville Salt Flats with no parachute brakes. Blue flame exhaust, the rocket fuel burns baby burns kind of dirty and bends the air. Seventy-, eighty-, ninety-plus-hour weeks, anything to feed the beast. John Henry hammering away to shore up the pittance those Amoco Eritreans were paying you, Jah Jah a go mash dem down, Black solidarity what, Black solidarity who? Your back, as predicted by Cassandra, firmly against the wall, what does idealism even mean when you're at the bottom with no clear path to the top and the world is against you and the bell starts to toll? Steal, plot, shoot, strong-arm, hustle, hoodwink, use, scam your way past the crab pack—why not?

They say that your grit, your hustle are precisely what this country's fabric is made of. That X marks your reserved spot within the melting pot. That you are cut from the same cloth. That everyone is welcome. That this land was mastered and made bountiful thanks to the strength of many who came just like you, persevered, joined forces, became unum. But there is what they say and there is what they do. There is what they preach and there is the truth. You just want to know: Is it *Come Together* or *Mississippi Goddamn*? And the answer, quizzically enough, is: both.

You think a little bit of things me go through, Trainer? In a new world but not of it. You must survive, adapt, strive, outwit. Old ways, new maze, no map, fresh eyes, new tricks. What do you throw? What do you keep? Which ones, among your values, your beliefs, your habits, your concepts, your understanding of things—will sink or swim? You've reached your destination but, inside of you, bewildering travels have barely begun. This place will forever change and rearrange you. No matter how prepared you think you are, no matter how ready,

47

your integrity will be assaulted, your strength questioned, your resilience tested; you will be shaken like a tree, stepped on like you're nothing; whether you thrive or not you will suffer, you will forswear yourself, you will reconfigure. Such is the lot of the displaced. It has nothing to do with being a Black man in a White man's land. That whole other set of problems swoops in slow and steady, acid droplets on bare melanin, tunnels inside flesh, holes through you as if you weren't even there, adding to the pile, insult to injury, pressing down on your shoulders, forcing your legs to buckle, stealing your stance, clouding your pride, challenging your right to exist, making you stumble further—wake up one morning and you're flimsy like a sieve, more empty space than fill. Yes, you're here, you've made it in. But even from the inside much remains out of reach. Ninety-nine percent of your time is carved out for work. So you don't enjoy the theaters and the museums, you don't take strolls in the summers, you don't sit on red checkered cloth atop grassy knolls, you don't rent kayaks from Georgetown Jack, you don't drizzle lemon juice on Marina seafood platters, you don't splash around the Dupont Hilton pool, you miss Gil Scott-Heron at the Blues Alley, and by the time you get your shit together Gil Scott-Heron has long been dead and gone, may God bless his tortured soul.

Didn't my people / Before me / Slave for this country? At least John Henry had his paperwork straight. You are among the illegals, the unseen, the marginals, the underground, the overworked, the overlooked, the underpaid, the wetbacks, the boat people, the downtrodden, the destitute, the cheated, the damaged goods, the exploited. You dutifully file your taxes and you follow the rules and you respect the law but you have no rights, you have no voice. E reminds you of that, too, when the two of you argue —the boys' school attendance, bedtime, sugar diet; the unending flow of visitors; the vanishing sex life; the missing collectibles and cash; the drugs in your midst; the footsteps in the dark—one single phone call, she reports you, they deport you. "It's that easy, baby. So don't tempt me, OK? Fuck you, and fuck those old shoes!" Oh, the shame…. What does it take? When is enough enough, with you?

N'a wan(n)de n'a sella, kon(n)gol bon(n)gol sellatâ—A wound will heal, a wicked word never.

You'd come this far just to live for E, made it to the big city only to lay it all at her feet. What was she supposed to do? She knew only what she knew: the dog-eat-dog, cold cold world of the towers; her parents absent and utterly useless; her babies' fathers uninvolved, uninvested and uninterested; her survival, and that of her offspring. And you—odd, communicative, complicated, emotional, sincere, sensitive, artistic, altruistic, hardworking, principled, caring, over-accommodating, naked armor, guard down, bleeding heart—threw her out for a loop. You matched none of her templates.

Forget ICE for a hot second, the Damocles sword E says is dangling over you. Puzzlingly enough, the fact that you've never hit her is also held against you. Damn if you don't, damn if you do.

49

Nothing wrong with a lovers' brawl, from her point of view. When she gets in your face and you don't push back, you don't slap or spit or punch or grab, she has this little smirk, she cuts her eyes, she pouts, she looks at you sideways, she wonders about you. Are you secretly gay or something, is there some hidden tendency you need to reveal, is she just for show, are you on some undercover brother bullshit? All her exes went to that body regularly, as expected, as normal, just the way it should be. Pulled her hair, pummeled her face, twisted her arms, bruised her boobs, cut her chin, kicked her shins, busted her lips. She never once called the police. When things get heated between the two of you, when her tone is off and she juts a finger and her tongue covers you in filth and mud and your blood gets roiled, you elevate, you reach for higher ground, you choose to take a deep breath and walk away. Who in the world does that? Your respect, your restraint, they are all wrong, they are too confusing. How does she know you love her with no limits, love her enough to beat her? How does she know she gets under your skin? Where's your fire? Were are your balls? Where are your nuts? What's in your guts? It's a warp. It's quite the twist. It's a mindfuck. It's a trip. Either way, you lose. Either way, you're toast.

"I got swag in the ass." Indeed, she does. And a cute face. And a nice set of all-American thighs. But pretty looks isn't all. But she can't cook and doesn't clean. But she never picks up a book. But she has no ambition. But the 10-year-old name-checks Yamamoto, Nigo, Saint-Tropez, Marant. But she was much nicer when you met her, more appreciative of you. Thin coat in the dead of winter, blizzard in the forecast, borrowed Reeboks; no heat, no food, no stamps, no Pampers, no stroller, no silver spoon. By summer's end she's already turned into somebody new, throwing shade like a total eclipse, giving you the blues. What do you do? Go and ask her to marry you.

E never bothered to veer off script. Understand where you were coming from and what you were trying to accomplish? Love you for who you were? Refuse what you so carelessly gave away? Shit, you were a custom-made zip line out of the projects. *You rob and gone / You gone with all of my loving / I said you rob and gone / You gone with all of my money.* So she, Rocksteady Queen, smashed and grabbed, strutted her stuff, straightened her body line, shook her shoulders, everything in time, dipped her hips, and took and took. Long after the dancehall emptied and the lights thrice flickered. Long after the selector packed up the 45s and scampered. Long after you stopped holding her interest. Long after she stopped giving a damn.

Your dreadlocks thinning and falling out. Your beard turning a not unbecoming psychosomatic gray. Your stomach churning with acid because she won't look you in the eye, her kisses are dry, her fingers are cold as asps and her thoughts lapse. *A man we passed / Just tried to stare me down.* Suspicious, jealous, restless, sleepless like an Appalachia methhead. *And when you cleared your throat / Was that your cue?*

Your dreams, this time around, a strident warning, fully exposing the maggots you do your best to whack-a-mole in the daylight, fresh apricot butter over your crumbling fruitcake. *Who is he? / And what is he to you?* E would candidly tell you of her infidelities. "I only feel satisfied when I cheat." Sitting next to her, you would shrink in place and become more and more transparent, deleted pixel by pixel, each word blotting out a part of your essence; you would feel not just a pain more ridiculous than anything you'd ever experienced, but insignificance, irrelevance, synchronous absence from the here and now and departure from yourself, near-total nothingness, Sartre suddenly making absolute sense. *We are spirits / In the material world.* You would try to speak, only to find out you couldn't utter a sound. Your face, in the morning, crusty with the tracks of tears, more salt you reap for the sterile Utah Flats. You asked for night and night E gave, now which way to the light? And, speaking of which, how come those were the only times you managed to cry? How deeply were your emotions buried inside—1,000, 10,000, 1,000,000 miles?

Bess, you is my woman now! You thought you were doing God's work. Helping, uplifting, breaking bread, spilling your own blood. Each one teach one. Isn't that what human beings are supposed to do? Love and care for one another? *They Shoot Horses, Don't They?*

The ghost town carousel carries you up and down and around and around. *And when I'm dead / If you could tell them this / That what was wood / Became alive.* Time a go dread, they say, and every gully a go run red. Time, they say, to separate the sheep from the wolves. Caught on the backend of that Redemption Song Tour? Intentions, they say, are the only things that really matter. Yours were always good, the plan deceptively simple: two souls, free will, a way, transmute trash into ore. If that ghetto crap taught you anything it's to be careful out there, to drive with both eyes and both hands, to never lose sight of yourself, to stop trying to save people. *D.C. / Don't stand for / Dodge City?* You begged to differ.

Ekkâde (n)gum(n)dan ina vêbi: mubbu gitama tan —It's easy to know what infatuation is: you only have to close your eyes.

Love is so many things. Perhaps too many, and more than most of us can handle at once. What it isn't is renouncement, sacrifice, forgoing your needs, peace of mind, safety—a zero-sum game. No pussy is ever that good. No sun has that much pull.

At least you got one great book out of all that morass and trickery, one chunky nugget out of the junk. The nerds will have their say. *Shine Eye Girl* rocks, even though the Immigrants Make America Great part remained safely tucked in the wings. Like all your near-misses, your past, your diagnostic, your bargains with the Devil. Guess it is nobody's business what you really went through, your life too surreal for fiction. I wouldn't have mentioned E and the boys in the Acknowledgements either, but that's just you, that's the type of person you are.

You can also thank E for your therapy. Alpha Lima Charlie Alpha Lima Yankee winging it up there for far too long—skids, low visibility, overbanking, headwinds, tailspins, missing components, pilot error, thruster malfunction, sabotage pure and simple, instrument panel calibration. Divorce as in-extremis ejection. Search and Rescue operation is a celebrity doctor with two offices and a weekly WPFW show. It is not, as Papa used to say, what we do; just the one thing you've believed all your life could truly help you. No insurance so you pay cash, Obamacare what, Obamacare who?

Your childhood, as announced in the action-packed preview, now playing on a screen near you. The doctor prompts, prods, prowls, never cajoles. Days good and bad or in between, like poking a long stick into literal and psychological silt. An arduous, fraught task. Progress and setbacks. It matters that she is who she is, that she also faced, and overcame, racism.

Walks you to the foot of the Spectrum, lets go of your hand. That's when the blurry part of your life ends. That's when the true work begins. Personality test: Who are you? Aptitude eval: Why do you do the things you do? Flight School for your bad habits. Maintenance for that workhorse of an engine.

Find yourself and E no longer is a problem. Venture off National Arboretum trails and practice screaming at the top of your lungs. You are Ta-Doow after all. You do own the motherfucker. Take off shirt to feel the sun and shoes to stomp the Earth. Weren't kings and warriors and boxers among your ancestors? Sleep naked to reawaken your sensuous side because *The Body Keeps the Score*. Run your fingers along arms and chest to revive skin sensation. Sit and breathe mindfully to thwart dissociation. Treat yourself to your very first longboard. Tricks of the trade, all.

You visit your friend the Atlantic at his Delaware home and relish the meeting, the crowds, the funnel cakes, and even, for once, the cold. You used to see yourself tumble down head first from high above, straight into the teeth of one of his more savage shores. You used to picture yourself jumping, falling, gone. In a cradle of rocks until the caressing fingers of waves washed you of the ultimate sin and dry blood. Lifted by the possessive arms of the tide. Pulled into the sarcophagus-like sanctuary of the deep. One with Old Man Atlantic. Silence and serenity. Done with the confusion, the loneliness, the suffering, the *sufferation*. Many days it came down to a fraction, the urge to finish it pressing you into action. What stopped you? You're not even sure. A sense of fairness, probably. A basic curiosity about the aftermath of your deeds. The notion that what represented the end for you would hollow out your family, destroy it from within. That you would take everyone with you. Your life was undoubtedly yours to dispose of. By choosing to terminate it, you bestowed upon your loved ones precisely the sort of all-encompassing, unending, overwhelming misery you sought to escape. Was that what they deserved?

You cry for the little boy you once were. The one you couldn't help. The one you tried so hard to forget. "I love you," you say over and over again. "I love you."

And it opens you up. And it melts you down. The knot between your shoulders stirs, loosens, untangles. The tension hunching your back dissolves. You now dream of thawing, reconnecting, rejuvenating, standing strong.

You must have been all but dead inside, and, without you noticing, it had to have transpired. "You look so alive!" says, à propos nothing, a random someone.

E throws you side looks, her power all but gone. Worry lines mar the normally impassive storefront. Your beautiful Frankenstein bride in retro pixie and sleeveless baby blue. Wedding vows what, wedding vows who? Where, her glorified puppet? Where, her certified fool? You can sense her desire, she who had you down for the count. It is both validating and unsettling. It makes you realize just how long it's been since she last wanted you, saw you for you, held your face between her palms to, soul to soul, stare deep into you. 1,000 absent suns suddenly reigniting, realigning, shifting, focusing, seeking to re-heat you. Play your cards right and the shop might just reopen. Sitting atop the pendulum as it swings, you hold off curtain and reverence, you wonder if this here comedy warrants a final act and the final act an encore, you can't help but turn and take one last long look back.

Does it matter that something should feel good if it doesn't feel right? Bitter / Sweet.

Hâra(n)dere rëwi ko demôwo—Satiation follows the farmer.

Golden is the harvest after extenuating, inhuman toil. You throw your corn and call no fowl. Crops of laughing berries, ripe mango, succulent peach, perky pomegranate, gorgeous apricot. You shoo the instigating snake away. "It's overdue," she says on the night of the repast, fluttering her eyelashes, batting back-to-back home runs, wooing you—you!

Ascending the glowing pyramid in your three-piece suit and diamond socks, Earth Shoes on your feet, every finger its shiny ring, you reminisce, you rise above Constant Spring. You smoke sweet sticky *sensi*, you think about E's big fat thing. Higher and higher you go, carrying treasure. Above the fray. Above the aches. Above the ashes of the fire that once burned bright, burned you good, totaled you. Stairs cut into the stone. Out of nowhere, a pink phoenix, the totem of these resurrection times. Flap-flap-flaps, leads the way. "She awaits," it says. "Do leave all encumbering baggage at the gate: the torment; the thoughts that intrude and hold back; your desiccated martyr heart." And so, eagerly, joyfully, freely, forgetfully, you climb. At the very top, billowing drapes line a festooned esplanade. A festival of flowers. Statues in pensive, revealing, evocative poses. Golden angels bearing her face. Horns of plenty. Waterfalls. Frolicking fish from every tropic inside dreamy ponds. Rococo pillars holding the clouds at bay. Exuberant rows of candles, flames oscillating in the jasmine breeze a solemn display. She is alone. You've traveled from the other side of the world to worship her. She stands, extends a hand. "Come closer." One long draw of the spliff for your nerves. She takes it from your fingers. Puff, she puffs, rights the vibe, nices it up—*irie ites*. Your present she impatiently unwraps. You hold your breath, hoping you still have got the touch. Pleased, she smiles, looks up. You exhale, walk toward the precipitous edge, proceed to throw it all to the wind —caution, nervousness, three-piece suit, Earth Shoes, diamond socks, diamond rings and things. You are naked, a blank slate, a new leaf. She is Aphrodite. Overdue, indeed. Her dress slips off her shoulders, falls at her feet. Her breasts are apples that she cups and offers, pagan goddess at the firmament, ruler of the temple. Nipples stems that you devour, a sigh of profound satisfaction escaping your lips. She is Salomé and you lose your head. She is Eve calling your name ever so softly, inviting you into the garden. "Eat." And you kneel. And you taste her. And she feeds you. She who over time became the most remote satellite, all but forbidden to you. This is how your deity atones, you see. No pledge of faithfulness everlasting, no remorse, no apology. Throbs with vital energy. Pulsates, glistens, parts ever so delicately. Takes you in, overwhelms you. From her cup, warm, thick, abundant, tangy honey. And it is delicious. *Madda*, *ditakh*, *koni*, *sideem*, *corosol*, *sapoti*. And you can't get enough. And it satiates your empty, starved, greedy vessel. She strokes your hair. She pokes the ashes. She sways. A hymn. She moans. "Eat." You flashback. Flash your locks. Natty Dread up on the mountaintop. You think, I've been here before. And your heart remembers the strophes, every lyric to the abandoned ode. And the goddess gently brings you to your feet, takes your hand and leads you to Paradise's door. The blaze that you both thought cold crackles, hisses, rises, sizzles. The baroque canopy bed has for columns four flambeau-bearing sculptures. Each scowl of twisted ebony you've seen before: Taz, Fonz, Smoke, D-Low. It is

60

she who now kneels and tastes you, her eyes never once letting go of you. She who then turns and faces the magnificent Versailles mirror, her gaze inscrutable. You let yourself fall behind her. She reaches back, guides you, brings you to her. You look on, reflection filling the frame of gilded bronze. She licks her lips. The goddess is hungry, too. Famished for you. "It's yours," she goads, her voice like rock on rock percussion. And you help yourself to her love. And you soar higher than ever before. And you marvel: Is this really E, who once enchanted me so? You pull her hair to catch every shout that escapes her throat. You bite her neck to mark the moment. *How do we know / From day to day / The sun is gonna rise?* And as you smack E's big fat thing again and again she stiffens, she stifles a yowl. Surprise / Delight. You raise your head to the Heavens, you let out a mighty roar. She *overstands*. No longer repressed. Never again denied. And, all around you, from the temple to the languid Constant Spring streets, never so ingratiating a whooshing and a rumbling sound—Babylon's walls cracking, crumbling, tumbling down.

Yes to second and third chances. From outmatched and outwitted to confetti and balloons. Tryst in the Amoco's backroom, belly dances like Istanbul, red-light revues like the Moulin Rouge. "I want you inside me." But when loving someone is akin to hating yourself, when the things hanging in the balance are your pride, dignity, self-respect, how low can you go, what choice do you really have?

Square, you've overhead one of the homegirls call you. African nigger, chimed another. Both in that

61

stupid accent, rough-hewn, inarticulate, downright ignorant, the one Black standup comedians reserve for immigrants from the Dark Continent, like a monkey singing a song, big eyes, big nose, big lips, big throat, big sound, pitch all over the scale, tone and inflection all off. So that is what they laugh about behind your back. That is what they think of when they think of you. Backwards. Dull. Slow. Unsophisticated. Unhip. Too dumb to see the circles E runs around you. "Biatch!" you say. All of them, E included. "Biatch!"

Kodida e 'aduna kala ma nettu—Everything in this world eventually comes to an end.

All this time, almost the entirety of your life together, E barely paid you any mind. You were the walls, the comfy chair, the 8 o'clock sitcom, the red Rihanna slippers; the tune she hummed in the shower; the everyday stuff she used and discarded without second thoughts; the robbery in progress, the multilayered scam, the elaborate heist, the slow-spreading paralysis, the drip of chest-constricting venom. Presence / Absence. How, despite all the ground regained, to ever come to terms with that?

"If anybody loved you, I and I did. If anybody held you high, it was I and I."

At the end of all the tweaking and retraining and repurposing, the runway beckons. You're feeling pretty good. The bird looks spanking new. Even the weather is all in—cloudy to fair, couldn't ask for more. Takeoff in ten. Due course, proper altitude, cruising speed, you steady your hand and fire the afterburner. Autism should have been on your radar.

Whenever the world was too much you always had music: verses rushing through to keep you calm and keep you sane, melodies a bridge to safety, arpeggios extracting you from the fear and confusion of gatherings. Statique is the first name the town gave you. Before the airplanes, space talk, and skateboards—way before Sabine. Maybe they meant the crepitations between radio stations; here but not here, annoying, meaningless, an anomaly, an unassigned destination, an unwanted slot, an empty frequency. Maybe they doubted you would ever evolve. Why doesn't he speak? He never mingles. Always locked in a room with some damn book and the stereo. Such a loser. Awkward. He's just plain arrogant. Lives in the clouds.

People thought what they thought and it was what it was. You were happy to stay inside your own head, bass and treble just so, riding the *riddim*, blasting off to some unexplored planet, charting custom-tailored paths through crocodile swamps and killing fields, the obstacle course that is everyday life. *What a bam bam / Bam bam bi lam.*

Songs did more than match your many moods. They were expression of emotions. They filled your chest with fireworks. They taught you how to process communication, translate feelings. Profession: wordsmith. Modus operandi: Acronyms as landmarks. Project: Map the world. So many walls you hit, so many rivers you crossed, Trouble Man you. *I came up hard / But now I'm cool / I didn't make it sugar / Playing by the rules.*

You wish that, growing up, you could have made those townsfolk understand that you mean well, that your oddities are just that—a mark of difference, not a threat. Too much activity, too many sensations coming at once, too much intensity and you go into a standstill, your circuits overload, your mind powers down. Nothing to do but function at reduced capacity while it all works itself out. Isolate yourself. Retreat. Travel backwards to the smallest of your superimposed Russian dolls, the inner core—call you Matryoshka. That you can be many places at the same time. That you've never met anyone quite like you, and had to blaze your own trail. That your kind of people typically doesn't stick around for very long. That your mind holds more words and music than it can possibly handle. That organizing and channeling this bounty into something creative and tangible will

64

be your life's work. That you found not one but several ways to be OK. That even though we all share this world, we each approach it in our own way. You wish that, back then, they'd been more accepting, and you less alone.

So clarity, hope, a better you. So two great outcomes out of one big fat L. Well, three if you count your Green Card. E never showed up for the marriage but she made it to the I.N.S. interview—she needed you in that new country of yours to keep on bankrolling her lifestyle. CREAM (Cash Rules Everything Around Me). YLYL (You Live and You Learn). GIWYFI (Get In Where You Fit In). RAW (Reciprocity Always Wins).

So Juliet. You hold her inside the idling Corvette and feel like the Chosen One all over again. You steal some of the warmth she so unselfconsciously radiates. You let your mind go. Lyrics, a bit corny if all too smooth, as only lyrics can be, hover around the edges:

I don't care where we go
I don't care what we do

And it is all actually pre-tty easy to conjure, it all rings way true: You already know the cinnamon of her lips, the call-and-response in her touch, the layered caramel of her skin. Multifaceted, endearing Juliet. Beats by the Backyard Band, marketing manual wedged between the seats, scented trees tangled in the rearview mirror—you know by now that, like mambo sauce and go-go music and New Balance 990s, it's a D.C. thing. Her eyes, tough or soft, sweet or fierce, lively or brooding; her short hair and nose of a *garçonne*. It's all comfortingly familiar.

Her nickname is Juicy J. She hails from Sierra Leone. She's been dancing since 16. She bites her nails, smokes cigarillos, calls her car Sweet Chariot—

as in *Swing down / I wanna ride / Swing down / I wanna ride.* She wants to be a one-man woman and settle down—just not right at this moment. She's good at what she does—stays in the gym, watches her carbs, analyzes her acts through and through, pampers her regulars, coddles her following. "My butt and boobs are real. I drive all the dope boys crazy." The money, too, is real—they make a show of carrying it into the club inside sneaker boxes, of throwing it in the air, of showering her with it night after night. So she worries about cashier's wrist, skin diseases, allergies, assaults, the I.R.S., and robberies. So she went and got her some Mace, a Glock, a Taser, a bill counter, an accountant, and a mad big safe. "The question is, Do I drive *you* crazy?" She spends it on her mom, Moschino, football jerseys, designer jeans, OG '97 Silver Bullet Air Maxes, and saves some for the next day. She knows her way around more than a pole. On the tip of her tongue, honeysuckle heat and passionfruit Alizé. She needs a slight push on slow nights and a big one on paid dates. Coke, X, herb, something stronger when the Devil so tempts her. She doesn't always do it for the dough. "For you, it'll always be free. Anything you want, I'll be." And you say to yourself, *We can deal with the rockets and dreams / But reality / What does it mean?*

Come on and touch
A place in me
That's calling out your name

She likes the overthinker in you, although her business acumen is lightyears ahead of yours. Sees herself go from five shows a week to four a month—rotating venues, standing-room only, heart-shaped center stage, professional lighting, rose petals, pyrotechnics, props, scripted numbers, a cut of both the door and the bar, one hundred percent of the merchandise booth, a four-digit markup on à la carte private sessions. And when that dries out or gets old, ideally before the 8-inch pumps and high-impact routines and nosebleeds and painkillers and lockers and hotel rooms all have conspired to pull up on her like thieves in the night, she'll go fully digital, move the Boom Boom Room behind a paywall: exclusive content, livestreams, lingerie, body molds, memoirs in downloadable installments—a sex-advice column, even. And, because it's a young woman's game either way, by the time that model also finds itself exhausted she will have ventured into something altogether different: talent management—a full-fledged agency, why not. She, too, dreams in technicolor. She, too, wants eternal sunshine, palm trees, panoramic views, off-white French patio doors, wraparound teal IKEA Billy bookcases, ("They deliver, you know?"), two kids, a pup and a swimming pool. She, too, wants to see California. You say, *And if we should / Live up in the hills?,* she says, "Huh huh, Pasadena or Laguna Beach. You write and I pay the bills. How does that sound, Daddy?"

> *We want each other*
> *Oh so much*
> *Why must we play this game?*

You get it. You dig her more than you show, more than she knows, more than you should. The fire in her veins. The wings beneath her feet. The thunder in her heart. Nowadays the tough questions come like a reflex's jaw—hard and fast and mean, and they don't let off, they don't relax, they don't let go: zero time to wallow in, contemplate, luxuriate. GIWYFI. Where, exactly, do you fit in? Would Maman and Papa understand, appreciate, tolerate? How much, if any, of the glamorous life can you handle? What of the hours, the pills, the blow, the spotlight, the stigma, the insecurity, the looks, the taunts, the stress, the creeps, the whispers? Can you share your girl with the whole wide world and still lock eyes with the man in the mirror? Your once-bitten shell-shocked post-traumatic heart refuses to sing. *You think a little bit of things me go through, Trainer?*

Through the windshield, beyond the trees, no swaying ribbons, no shimmering silver letters. It is to your ancestor Battling Siki that you turn, for once. Because all the others are mum on matters of the heart? Because life is a match in 12 rounds? Because love is a losing game? Because you once knew a girl named Sabine? Because perspective, hindsight, and revisionism since have you wondering about her, her mom, and Mr. Internationalist himself, the Marlboro Man? Regrets are a motherfucker.

Your teenage years so far yet so fresh. You now know a thing or two. Time is neither friend nor foe. It just is. Dragons, of the kind that stalked Sabine, of the kind that tortured you, are not *sui generis*. They are the spawns of sins, reactions to an evil act, bruises to a young defenseless psyche, manifestations of a transgression; the ultimate unedited uncensored origin story; a circle completing itself in a ring of fire. TMNF. Where were you when Sabine needed you?

"I'm so cold," says the postcard from assignment in yet another exotic location. "I'm cold without you." Your old flame now stuck in winter. No matter where she goes, it's never warm enough. "Nothing like Africa's sun," she adds, as if it is as simple as that, as

70

if she doesn't have a condition, as if this isn't the Archipelago messing with her mind, keeping her in its grip, completing the karmic 360. When she says she misses you, does she really mean you or just what used to join the two of you—the connection, the feeling, the glue? How much of the past is ever left over for us to recapture? She casts her lines but you won't bite. Passes from too far upfield to rush and catch.

You don't always respond. Somehow she always finds you. Now writes full time, not just to you. Call her Capote, too. All that fashion stuff and arts school got her into documentary filmmaking and shorts at Studio Canal+, just the kind of charmed life she destined herself to. Bumping into Prince at the New Morning in Paris—"He is sooo short!" Dropping by Ruben and Isabel Toledo's Manhattan atelier. Telling Christophe Lambert in Giorgio Armani's Milan villa she started calling you Fred after *Subway*. You reminisce about those days—tan trench coat, holes in your 501s' knees, blue on blue Odysseys, briefcase for your cassettes when you deejay, punk for life or is it goth or dark-edged pop, *Never thought tonight could be / This close to me.*

The message in those anecdotes is aha! and almost cliché: You peaked early, she's ascending. No longer birds of one feather, friendly skies together. Sierra Alpha Bravo took a long nosedive but stuck her landing. And the crowd roars.

When you were young and things were good the two of you always talked of escaping to your own

71

deserted island. As if you weren't alone enough. As if the bubble wasn't bubble enough. You wanted no intrusion, suffered no interruption. *Là-bas ne seraient point ces fous / Qui nous disent d'être sages.* You imagined a space just for two, where life is a beach and you never die, the weather kind and Nature provides, storms only bring more warmth, the peace and shelter you offer each other go on and on and on and forever. How many have experienced such fulfillment? Say the word and Sabine was willing to go. How lucky were you?

Sometimes the postcards are downright angry and you wonder, Who are you today; Who are you right now? We were only children, Sabine. We were only children, back then. It's easy to blame me for everything that went wrong. Maybe it's the fact that I know so much, that you went too far without a commensurate payload, that you didn't get back what you put in. Welcome to the club, is what I have to say. *Stop the fuss / Stop the fight.* You're all right.

Often we are mere bystanders in someone else's drama. Often we also are mere bystanders in our own. Unless.

When our time is ended / How will we have spent it?

Siki. My Siki. Oftentimes your courage borders on recklessness. So big it fills a whole arena with awe. Fight just to fight, you seem to say. Fight unprepared, untrained, uninformed, overweight. In Dublin against an Irishman on St. Patrick's Day. A greedy dog for manager, fingers of whiskey to defibrillate you from a knockout, corner men dabbing your eyes with the same filthy rag round after round, an opponent whose punches send oodles of your blood high in the smoky air, a crowd that cheers or boos just the same. Go for it, you never stop to say, your grin crooked, your gaze merry. Grab life by the neck. Ride that bitch til the end of the Earth. The world is yours.

All I want is to spend the night together
All I want is to spend the night in your arms

Your poor little post-traumatic heart. *Natty never get weary*, Joseph joyously sang, yet here you are. *Oh Jah Jah / Oh Jah Jah / Take him where life sweeter*. So many trips down Heartbreak Road. So many laps on that wretched merry-go-round. Wasted. All wasted. Through your fingers like Sahara sand.

"Requirements," Anaëlle famously suggested. You close your eyes and let the word hit you. You take a deep breath and wonder what it could mean for someone like you. This is another way you've discovered how to learn: When people you've come to trust—people better adjusted and attuned to the world—teach you.

Here is Juliet, the end of your shift and a little before hers. *Cosmic Girl* Part II. The soul in her kisses transports you. She makes you feel. And it can all be so simple, right? Magnetize, make out on a space bed, lace his and hers Silver Bullets, take the party over to Star One. You've never even seen her dance. You're not sure you want to. Either way, the Boom Boom Room is not for you: Booties twerking and G-strings popping, more boobs than bombs over Baghdad, dollar bills stacked to the ceiling, rapid-fire changing lights, you'll be the guy hugging the five-ton speaker to no avail, you who've never met a song you couldn't sneak into, the people and noise and raunchiness enough to make you lose your mind, no friendly chords, no safety in the pocket, nothing to lasso in, ride out, latch onto, utter sensory hell with no defensive line, jukes out of whack, sack after sack after sack, for your distress no lifeline—*It's time for the Percolator! / It's time for the Percolator! / It's time for the Percolator!*

Some things never change. They call her Juicy J. That's enough knowledge for you. *And the ride / The ride / Is so sweeeet*. You hold the cards close to your chest, for once. You hold the key. You know you do. The clock, it keeps on ticking and ticking. That's the sound of life inexorably passing by you. No extension, second helpings, OT or Hail Mary. The odds, you know, are nowhere near the minimum. Never a gambling man so gun-shy.

And the gods laugh. And the crowd frets.

Once upon a time you lived on Mount Olympus. How cool are you? You now possess downfield vision. Given another chance, yesterday will only break your heart—again. Under California's money-green skies Juliet's 350 horses will freely roam, lecherous knights carry her throne. The good life.

Many many years ago you left your home in search of fortune and wisdom. Called yourself Prodigal Son. *Exodus / Movement of Jah people.* I and I came to conquer? The /th/ sound stubbornly stomps you. Your hopes recede further with every moment that flies and every turn that blinds. You still can't sing. Didn't learn the guitar. Got too old before you got good enough to make it skating. Never did become a pilot. Whether your stories will be just the thing to carry you into hyperspace remains to be seen.

Where, the feast you were promised? Where, the pot of gold? Where, the baby boy called Nate? What you found is hard to pinpoint, came at great cost, and still nowhere worth what you've lost. Scant to show for your struggles abroad. Sneakers for your fetish, books for your soul, LPs for your Congo synthetic rubber plantation; a whole bunch of football metaphors; calluses, scars, bittersweet memories you call your own.

Anaëlle is getting married. Should you have asked her to wait for you? It wasn't that type of relationship; she wasn't that kind of girl. Part of you did hope she'd have kept her night light on in case you wished to return. We all pine, at wits' end, for a star mapping the way back. Everybody wants their cake and eat it, too. Everybody wants their Cassiopeia.

So you tread on. In a faraway seaside abode, the waters are rising and your parents slowly getting old. Nothing, they assure you, that a good marabout can't get a fix on. It lingers on your mind days after you hang up the phone. And the country, oh your poor country....

Anaëlle visits your family, like the dutiful daughter-in-law she could have become. Over *baasi saleté*—the couscous masterpiece adorned with white beans, tomato sauce, chunks of beef, dates, yams, manioc, carrots, eggplant, and cabbage— shared on the shaded patio, Maman reveals what happened to you. "She was crying," Anaëlle tells you. "So was I. I'm so sorry. I had no idea what you went through. That little. That early."
You close your eyes, repress a sob. "That stuff doesn't run my life any more," you say, Maman and Anaëlle's tears like a balm over the wounds of long ago. "It used to, though."

You hear that the youth are more agitated than ever. Resignation? They'd rather burn and loot than bow their heads and drink mint tea, sit on the waiting list of aid groups, turn on one another for scraps and tools. Moving, yelling, running from the police and shoot-to-kill soldiers, hurling bricks, dodging bullets, you feel less hungry, more alive. Lost Generation what, Lost Generation who? They're just like you. Going against the grain. Rolling the dice. Going for broke. Pawning the family home or village parcel for a one-way ticket to a place they've never seen, a tomorrow nowhere near guaranteed. Unsafe passage to the nearest Spanish spit of sand or rock-strewn beach. Lifejackets, Dramamine, swimming lessons, satellite phones a maybe. Midnight bus on the thousand-year-old Salt Road, last stop Tichit. Foot trek on dunes stretching as far as the eye can see. Find the holes in borders, cross the invisible lines in the sea. Kindness, disposition of spirit of the receiving parties remaining to be seen. For the lucky few who happen to make it, a new status, hard-won privileges: modern-day slaves in Italian olive groves or the luxury garment industry, tears in your vinaigrette, blood on your Gucci; extra-judicial detention in Libyan militia-run facilities; nannies in Marseille; prostitutes in Prague; dishwashers in Bonn; *bana bana* on the Riviera. If they happen to grow fond of their Promised Land / Rainbow Country it won't be from opportunity, deep acquaintance, or passing enjoyment, but because time and routine will have done what they do. Grace will lift their spirits at unexpected moments. They'll find solace in odd places, contentment in labor, sleep in exhaustion. The Universal will bless them with its wisdom—no adaptation needed, no reintroduction: rays of light that trickle through a basement window at the perfect moment; fresh peanuts on display in a chain store international section; cowry shells on a little brown-skinned girl; summers like the thick of rainy season;

the grind of wheels and the flip of boards, hooded skaters circling a tucked-away mezzanine like winged riders come nightfall. They'll pick one of their most destitute customers and try to save her—eenie, meenie, miny, moe—and then they'll wait, and wait, for her to hold the elevator, turn around and save them in return. She'll be the kind to never say what she means and never mean what she says and never mind what she does. So they'll need to develop extra-sensorial faculties in order to beat Babylon at its own game. As they struggle to remain whole, guardian angels will pledge silence; their families will Indiana Jones jinns down rabbit holes and smuggle boxes of powders and prayers and potions through hypervigilant customs; their friend the sidewalk peddler will look on with sorrow and mercifully stop short of I told you so. They will fail, even though failure is not an option; they will hide to curl up and hang their head down low, and maybe then, maybe then, maybe then tears will flow. Africa doesn't eat its own? But check this out: *Ko démma dûti wö, vêtai*— No matter how long the night, day will surely come. They will get up and face the horror, screwface back on, Pretender, Pretender. iPod in the left pocket, Kindle in the right. Because there's a shift to cover. Because the game is about more than treason, callousness, wickedness, badness, and bad blows. *Dreadie's got a job to do / He's got to fulfill that mission / He will survive / In this world of competition.*

We seek what we seek: a little dignity; bootstraps to propel ourselves up the ladder of Humanity. No one knows how man's deepest longings unfold.

So SSDD. Discipline was never a problem; balance is. You go to work and return home to write late into the night. Wake up and go to work. Go home and write. About what was and what wasn't. What could have been. What will be if people like you, and Anaëlle, have their say. You write about your family: the Conqueror, the King, the Saint, the Merchant, the Boxer, the Agrégé, the Beauty. Everything else, you got out of your system. There's enough there to fill your space in its entirety. You stay focused. You stay busy.

"I wonder if Kantouri is still open," you muse before zipping up your coat, pulling your hood up, dashing out into the cold. A Groundhog Day kind of night. Solo bus ride, a little writing if the spirit so moves you.

And, in the blink of an eye, zero for four as Juliet, too, is lost to you.

You search the sky for signs of the earthbound storm. Not lonely by any means; just alone. As a buffer against the pain that is slowly but surely seeping back in, you grab a shovel and you start digging, and digging. The exercise brings you no small amount of happiness. "Positives to fight negatives," is what the doctor recommended. So you dig, you dig away. You shadow box. You train for Fight Night, you spar for Bout Day.

When the hole is deep enough, you jump in, you bury yourself in research, you pepper Papa with questions about the past.

"At least we could see," he begins. "And they transferred to us all but the most top-secret files. Unlike in Conakry. 'We prefer poverty in liberty to riches in slavery,' is what Sékou Touré told de Gaulle in '58. So the French took everything of value with them and destroyed the rest. Mounds of objects, machines, engines, appliances big and small, all broken beyond repair. Everything systematically thrown in heaps in the middle of the street and doused with gasoline. Same way they used to burn our crops and poison our wells during the time of conquest. Had they had the leisure, they would have dropped a bomb on every single building, every bridge, every road. Imagine taking over a country in figurative and literal darkness: bare offices, smashed furniture, busted windows; no records, no paperwork, no training manuals, no books; no pencils, no paper, no typewriters, no lightbulbs; no medicine, no equipment, no tools, no supplies, no cash reserves, no assets, no fuel. How do you ever manage?

"Our own transition was rather smooth. We could sit, make phone calls, consult archives, educate ourselves in the inner workings of government, keep the affairs of the State going, start steering the ship our way. We had continuity. But our modern-day story really begins with two men: the Politician and the Technocrat.

"The Politician was suave and savvy, if outwardly meek. He was a man of letters who had gone to prestigious French schools and universities. He believed, somewhat naively, that even after achieving autonomy West Africans should maintain close economic and cultural ties with France. The Technocrat was a man of the people, deeply committed to the countryside. He was pragmatic, rigorous, austere, and hardworking. Both men shared a basic sense of integrity and a vision of Socialism tailored to their country.

"The new Constitution, administration, and institutions were all directly adopted from the Fifth Republic. In the rush to placate the old masters, critical mistakes were made that trapped us in a neocolonial embrace for decades. The French made several demands that would leave them embedded into the inner workings of all sectors of activity, and in a position to quickly intervene militarily: To maintain combat-ready troops inside a handful of bases on our now sovereign soil; to coordinate defense; to consult with France before any major Foreign Policy decision; to keep French advisors close to the presidency, and technical assistants in each ministry; to bind our national currency to the Franc; to guarantee French businesses and settlers equal rights to our citizens; to never nationalize French firms; to offer government-backed guarantees to French investors.

"The Technocrat urged caution. The Politician readily agreed to all the clauses. So it really was a transition that wasn't: The French alone possessed market-ready goods, capital, the know-how and personnel to operate the factories. It was obvious that the economy as a whole would firmly remain in their hands, giving them leverage to control the political life of their former colony as well.

"'I was completely subjugated by him,' the Technocrat would later confess. 'I was like his *talibé* —his disciple.' The two became friends in 1948, when he was a teacher known for his militant ideas and devotion to the peasantry, and the Politician one of a handful of deputies of color in the French Parliament. The Politician became the new country's first President. The lion that came to represent our nation is his father Diogoye's emblem, as well as a symbol of courage, loyalty, and strength. The green in our flag signifies hope. He composed the National Hymn. Despite his deep distrust of politics, the Technocrat agreed to oversee the new administration and hold the Defense portfolio, effectively becoming the most powerful man in the State.

"Freed of the day-to-day task of running the country, the Politician turned to publishing world-acclaimed poetry, cultivating special-interest groups, and promoting Négritude, a concept incomprehensible to all but the most philosophically inclined. The Technocrat worked wholeheartedly on agricultural reform with the goal of lifting the countryside out of poverty. His development program, called '*Animation Rurale*,' attempted to break the monopoly of powerful marabouts and foreign-born middlemen on the cultivation and sale of peanuts, the country's chief economic engine. Villagers were organized in cooperatives to which a newly created state bank offered loans, and homegrown scientists lent expertise. The Technocrat immersed himself in paperwork and statistics. Toured all corners of the country by plane to inspect everything himself—fields, equipment, even the books—outfitted in a cowboy hat and sunglasses. In less than two years, the cooperatives' output represented seventy-five percent of the national market.

"Emboldened, he turned his focus to other nation-building concerns: ridding the country of French soldiers and advisers—the so-called Technical *Insistence*; stemming the corrupt proclivities of government officials by forbidding them to participate in or own business ventures; curbing the growing influence of French union syndicates over the urban workforce; introducing formal Arabic studies into the schools curriculum in the long-term goal of reducing the grip of the marabouts over civic discourse and spiritual life. 'Reined in—all of them!' he celebrated, a bit prematurely.

"*Hautare ko halkare*—Presumption is perdition.

"He was a man of exceptional drive, intelligence, and honesty. In his hurry to uplift the masses, he ruled mostly by decree, circumventing Parliament. His concept of a modern, egalitarian, fluid, Islamic society went further than Négritude. His downfall was his relative lack of sophistication in matters of politics and human nature, his refusal to play the game. In a morally bankrupt landscape, austerity, brashness, and rectitude are fatal liabilities. If nothing else, Lumumba's recent assassination should have served as a warning.

"The cabal against him started within his own administration—simply put, a bevy of fine gentlemen were ready to eat, and he stood in their way. The pretext was abuse of power.

"The Politician had the ear of the French government and private business interests, the marabouts and their supreme leader, the *Khalifa*. Most importantly, he had the backing of the army, his and the French.

"'I had to arrest him before he arrested me,' the Politician declared from the Palace rooftop on Christmas Eve, 1962, tears streaming down his face. Down at the Chamber of Commerce, they sabered bottles of Champagne. The Technocrat was hastily convicted of treason and condemned to lifetime imprisonment. He was taken to a newly built jail in one of the hottest parts of the country, in the Oriental Region hinterland; kept in total isolation; given a lemon tree to plant; and forced to dig his own grave.

"Gone, agricultural reform, self-sufficiency, the empowerment of the peasant class. In their stead, foreign loans; debt-heavy, graft-laden infrastructure projects; bloated civil sector; reduced public spending; economic stagnation. When it came, the drought quickly pushed us over the edge.

"While the nation floundered, the Politician became more and more detached from reality, honing his literary credentials, spending the majority of his time in Normandy.

"The Technocrat was freed on humanitarian grounds after 12 years of solitary confinement. Half blind, frail, prematurely aged, he burst into tears upon realizing what had become of his beloved homeland —the waste, the scramble for riches, the 'new dependencies.'

"We had such a great start," Papa laments. "We were an example to the whole of Africa. All squandered away. For what? Thirst for power. Egoism."

Mundo dei ˊaduna—He who is patient will rule the world.

The two coalesced slowly, like all good things. Almost becoming one, pulverizing your forever complacency, pushing you to the limit; so that, in the end, you were forced to make your move: nostalgia for country; surefire feelings for a girl. You think about it on your way to reclaim both. You think about it on the plane home.

Growing up, you relished taking roadtrips to the countryside. Maybe because the atmosphere inside the city seemed to always be stuffy, tense, busy, things at home borderline melancholy. Maybe because immediately past Rufisque the landscape began to open up, turning green like a promise and trappings-free, if a bit scrawny, the one-lane road alternately cutting through dense and sappy *neem* forests or imperturbable, immutable savanna. Malika Beach was a favorite picnic spot, unfit for swimming because of strong currents but cool and peaceful under a canopy of *filao* trees. It became so endearing to Papa that he would eventually acquire conjoined parcels close by. There, he cleared the brush with an old Fiat bulldozer and held back the dunes and saltwater with a handful of deep wells coupled to pumps, and a rudimentary irrigation system. Mango and coconut trees were planted for fruit and shade. On clearly delineated, if tiny, rectangular plots, he then grew, among other things, corn, potatoes, onions, lettuce, tomatoes, mint, the inevitable peanuts, and *kani*, the native variety of red pepper prized for its fieriness—an intellectual giving in to his love for the land, a doctor turned weekend farmer in Afro, short sleeves, bluejeans, babouches, severe but stylish Mobutu glasses; a novice trying his thumb at coaxing greenery out of sand and sun. Trial, and, for the most part, error, testing his mettle, taxing Maman's patience, stretching the family's finances.

On longer outings you would first cover the 30 km or so to Diamniadio, the crossroads from which either Route Nationale led to grandparents' homes: N2, following the coast all the way north to Saint-Louis, the fading river town near Mauritania where Maman was born; N1, crossing the country from west to east, kissing Papa's birthplace in the sultry center near the Gambian border before reaching toward Mali. There was togetherness in those excursions; the joy of being a family; the anticipation of visiting relatives. Papa loved cars, and would go on to own quite an assortment, all purchased secondhand, only the most recent in working order. He drove fast and remained alert, ready for anything untoward like unruly cattle, horse-drawn carts, overcrowded bush taxis, Saviem and Volvo eight-wheelers piled so

87

haphazardly with jute or sisal sacks of hay, coal, or rice, they would tip to the side. Maman relaxed in her seat, visor down, sundress a splash of gaiety, her hair in a loose ponytail, her face behind sunglasses. In the backseat, you and your siblings either played or read or looked out the window or bickered like all siblings do, thoughts expanding with the vistas, hearts full. Something in the mood just lifted.

Thus also presented itself the opportunity for perspective, suffused by the dichotomy between the cosmopolitan dame on Africa's westernmost tip and the underdeveloped interior. Like leaving one world to enter something lesser, incomplete, unfinished, neglected, forgotten. Like traveling back in time. There was nothing outside the capital and a few regional centers for most people to subsist on. Stop anywhere along either Nationale and the car would be rushed by barefoot and half-naked children, stoic young women offering local wares. The men mostly held back, a little more reserved, a touch more proud. You were an event, a break from the boredom, a reprieve from the monotony. It didn't take much to imagine their lives, their homes. They lacked everything: food, running water, electricity, paving, public sanitation, education, training, healthcare, work, solid walls, a decent roof. Whether you had stopped to purchase something from a roadside stall or just to stretch your legs and exchange a few words, there was never any unpleasantness in those interactions. Curiosity, yes. Nothing, on the villagers' part, to suggest resentment or bitterness, revolt, anger against their lot. It drove home a few important points: these were your people; you were immensely privileged; you must, at some moment in the future, like Papa before you, report for duty, do your part, bring your piece to the *casse-tête*, help solve the big development puzzle. It struck you sometimes that these were things no one outside your family spoke about. No one but Anaëlle. As it turned out, this would, for the two of you, become more than enough common ground. She is the one person who, once you came of age, went farther than brief encounters by the Nationale. She stepped inside the postcards; she put a name on some of those unseen villages; she assessed their situation; she tried to address their problems.

Dîdube hâdu (n)den(n)di sago—Those who share needs are united in desire.

Africa and Anaëlle. If we all leave never to return, within whose hearts will the struggle ferment, and, ultimately, leap from? Give you Ferlo, Jolof, Walo, Baol, Cayor. Give you the red dust that blows from up North. Give you El Haj Omar, Albouri, Cheikh Anta. Give you Ismaël Lo, Xalam II, Super Diamono, Baba Maal, *Camp de Thiaroye*. Give you projectiles for the barricades and propellant for the Molotovs. Give you kalashnikovs for the Presidential Guard and C4 for the Palace doors. Give you a start from scratch instead of indignities abroad, those Western Union remittances of blood. Give you the luck of the draw, triumph over your rival in matrimony. Give you a lifetime of rainy seasons with Anaëlle, who graced you with the space to find your purpose. Give you many more years with Papa, Maman, your sisters, your brother.

And even this could have been foretold: Where else, when it's all said and done, do you truly belong? Cruising the azure, Old Man Atlantic winking, nodding in approval, shimmering in turquoise down below. In the place receding from your horizon they're killing Black people like 1860s open season. "Biatch!" you say. You've picked your battle. You're going home.

"I have two loves," you confess on down the road. "You and Fouta Toro."

"As long as I'm number one," Anaëlle laughs, "you'll always have us both."

That habit of yours, your propensity to hear what's not here. Your flights of fancy, your galloping mind, your auditory imaginings. "I'm pregnant," is what your forever friend has just revealed, hitting you like a ton of bricks, crushing you like a head-on collision. "I'm expecting his son." Just then your phone rings, and you try to ignore it, but it gets incessant, it gets annoying, and when you take a look, the Caller ID says Emergency System Shutdown Imminent, and you know just what it means, and there's a burst of heat and a flash of white light. But you hold on tight. You exit stage right. You don't get the girl in the end, you don't get what you thought, you don't even get to fight. And it sucks. And it hurts. And it is, also and however and above all, the first time you really really want what you want. Zero for four you may still be. No slack from the scoreboard. But you've learned to crave, to thirst, to lust, to desire, to wish desperately, to deliberately sink your teeth into the prize, to work those jaws and steal a bite. Smile. Do your dance. Pat yourself in the back. Get back in the game. You are alive. You still have a country to save.

Adapted from the upcoming novel "Yesterday Will Break Your Heart."

Contains excerpts from the following, in order of appearance, all used without permission, some repeatedly.

"Take Me With U" Prince & the Revolution
"Pretender" Matumbi
"Look at Us Now" Alexander O'Neal
"The Message" Grandmaster Flash and the Furious Five
"When Doves Cry" Prince & the Revolution
"Freddy's Dead" Curtis Mayfield
"Nasty Girl" Apollonia 6
"A Fool Will Fall" The Wailing Souls
"Your House" Steel Pulse
"The Ballad of Dorothy Parker" Prince & the Revolution
"Sometimes It Snows in April" Prince & the Revolution
"Back to Love" Evelyn King
"Salomon Sang" Cassandra Wilson
"Reality Poem" Linton Kwesi Johnson
"If You Were Here Tonight" Alexander O'Neal
"Who Is He And What Is He to You" Bill Withers
"Love Is Blindness" Cassandra Wilson
"Are You My Baby" Wendy & Lisa
"Trainer" Michael Smith
"Crazy Baldheads" Bob Marley & the Wailers

"Don't Dream It's Over" Crowded House
"Rob and Gone" Barrington Levy
"Rocksteady" Alton Ellis
"Spirits in the Material World" The Police
"Porgy and Bess" George & Ira Gershwin
"Wooden Horse" Suzanne Vega
"D.C Don't Stand for Dodge City" The Go-Go Posse
"Three Piece Suit" Trinity
"Don't Worry" Sanchez
"Bam Bam" Sister Nancy
Trouble Man" Marvin Gaye"
"Mothership Connection" Parliament Funkadelic
"Man in the Hills" Burning Spear
"Close to Me" The Cure
"Une Île" Jacques Brel
"Stop the Fuss" Horace Andy
"Never Get Weary" Culture
"Biko" Steel Pulse
"A Funky Space Reincarnation" Marvin Gaye
"Percolator" Cajmere
"Little Red Corvette" Prince & the Revolution
"Exodus" Bob Marley & the Wailers
"Ride Natty Ride" Bob Marley & the Wailers

Printed in Poland
by Amazon Fulfillment
Poland Sp. z o.o., Wrocław

27591918R00054